# Georgie
## the Royal Prince
## Fairy

To Hamish Field, with love

Special thanks to
Rachel Elliot

ORCHARD BOOKS
338 Euston Road, London NW1 3BH
Orchard Books Australia
Level 17/207 Kent Street, Sydney, NSW 2000
A Paperback Original

First published in 2014 by Orchard Books

HIT entertainment

A CIP catalogue record for this book is available
from the British Library.

ISBN 978 1 40833 064 7

1 3 5 7 9 10 8 6 4 2

Printed in Great Britain

The paper and board used in this paperback are natural recyclable
products made from wood grown in sustainable forests. The
manufacturing processes conform to the environmental regulations
of the country of origin.

Orchard Books is a division of Hachette Children's Books,
an Hachette UK company

www.hachette.co.uk

# Georgie
## the Royal Prince
## Fairy

by Daisy Meadows

ORCHARD

www.rainbowmagic.co.uk

The Fairyland Palace

Wetherbury Docks

Queen's Palace

Jack Frost's
Ice Castle

Wetherbury Village

Kirsty's House

Racecourse

Jack Frost's Spell

I will make the fairies suffer.
I will be a ruthless King!
I will stop those pesky humans,
When I have the golden ring.

Then my frost will kill the summer.
Then the icy bells will peal.
All of Fairyland will freeze,
When I possess the royal seal!

# Contents

# The Royal Weekend

"Rachel, are you awake?" whispered
Kirsty Tate.

It was an early Saturday morning in
Wetherbury, Kirsty's home town, but this
was not an ordinary weekend.

"Yes, I've been awake for hours. I'm
too excited to sleep!" Rachel Walker
replied. "Can you believe we're going to
see three real princes today?"

"And we're actually going to meet them at the palace garden party tomorrow," added Kirsty with a happy sigh. "It's like a dream, isn't it?"

Rachel hopped out of bed and opened the curtains. The summer sun was already making the dew sparkle on the grass outside. She climbed into bed beside her best friend.

"But I'm also excited about the ship launch and the races," Kirsty added.

The whole country had been talking about the royal weekend for months. The Queen had invited three royal princes from other countries to stay for the weekend. Children from all over the nation had been invited to a special children's garden party at the palace, and Rachel and Kirsty were included.

"I think Dad is most looking forward to the launch of the ship," said Rachel. "And Mum is really excited about wearing her new hat at the races."

Wetherbury was close to the palace, so Rachel and her parents were staying with the Tate family for the weekend.

"It's going to be a busy day," said Kirsty. "Mum said we have to leave early to make sure we get a good view of the ship launch."

"Yes, and then we have to rush to catch the train to the racecourse," Rachel remembered. "What time does the royal race start?"

Kirsty didn't reply. She just gave Rachel a gentle nudge with her elbow, and then nodded over at her bedside table. The night before, they had been playing princesses, and they had left Kirsty's pretend tiara lying on the bedside table. It was only made of plastic, but now it was glimmering as if it were made of real diamonds.

12

"It looks like fairy magic!" said Rachel with a smile. Then the girls heard a tiny laugh like a babbling brook, and a beautiful fairy sprang out from behind the tiara. She twirled across the bedside table and then sank into a deep curtsey.

"Hello, Rachel and Kirsty," she said in a low, musical voice. "I'm Georgie the Royal Prince Fairy."

The best friends squeezed

each other's hand. A visit from a fairy
made the weekend absolutely perfect!
Kirsty and Rachel had been friends
of Fairyland for a long time, and they
had always kept the magical secret
between them.

"Hello, Georgie!" said Rachel. "It's
lovely to meet you."

"I'm very happy to meet you both at
last," said Georgie. "I've heard of all the
wonderful things you have done to help
Fairyland, and Kate the Royal Wedding
Fairy told me how you saved her True
Love Crown from Jack Frost."

Georgie rose into the air and fluttered
over to perch on the end of Kirsty's bed.
She was wearing a pretty polka-dot shift
dress and sparkling shoes. A golden tiara
was tucked into her shining blonde hair.

"I look after all princes in the fairy and human worlds," Georgie explained. "I'm here today to give you a special invitation."

She flicked her wand and a magical scroll unfurled in the air. As the girls watched, they saw golden writing appear on the scroll.

Dear Rachel and Kirsty,

Princess Grace and Prince Arthur are proud to announce the birth of their beautiful baby son.

You are invited to celebrate with them on Sunday at the royal naming ceremony.

RSVP

The girls gave gasps of delight.

"That sounds wonderful!" said Kirsty. "We'd love to come, wouldn't we, Rachel?"

"Definitely!" said Rachel with a beaming smile. "This is turning into a very royal weekend indeed!"

Georgie laughed.

Suddenly, Kirsty had a horrible thought.

"What about Jack Frost?" she asked. "I bet he'll try to do something nasty to spoil the ceremony!"

# Georgie's Surprise

"What do you mean?" asked Georgie.

"The human world has lots of stories about bad-tempered enemies casting spells on royal babies," Kirsty explained, thinking of Sleeping Beauty.

Georgie gave another bubbling laugh.

"Those are just bedtime stories, Kirsty," she said. "The baby prince is perfectly safe from Jack Frost. The Ice Lord is

coming to the ceremony, and he has been strutting around talking about royalty all day long. I think he wishes that he were royal too!"

Kirsty still felt a bit uneasy. After all, everyone knew that Jack Frost could not be trusted. But Georgie seemed to be sure that everything would go well, so Kirsty decided to forget about her worries.

"I'll come and collect you on Sunday afternoon, after the garden party at the palace," said Georgie.

"We're really looking forward to it," Rachel replied. "Thank you for bringing the invitation!"

Georgie gave them a little wave. Then she disappeared in a flurry of tiny, glittering crowns, which faded away after a few seconds. Rachel and Kirsty looked at each other and let out little squeals of excitement.

"This is going to be the best weekend ever!" said Rachel. "Come on!"

They jumped out of bed and started to get ready for the day.

But as they were brushing their hair, there was a flash of twinkling lights and Georgie appeared on the bedside table again. This time, she wasn't smiling and her cheeks were pale.

"Oh, girls, something awful has happened," she cried. "While I was visiting you earlier, Jack Frost stole my special royal seal!"

"That's terrible," said Kirsty. "But what exactly *is* the royal seal?"

"It's a golden ring with a special pattern engraved on it," Georgie explained. "It's a really important part of all naming ceremonies for princes, because I use it as a stamp to complete the naming certificate."

"Why does Jack Frost want it?" asked Rachel.

"Because he wants to rule over Fairyland as King Jack," said Georgie. "The seal is very powerful, and he knows that he can use its magic to make him royal. If we don't find the royal seal before Sunday afternoon, the naming ceremony will be cancelled, and the newborn prince won't have a name!"

Rachel and Kirsty were horrified.

"We have to do something!" said Kirsty.

"Queen Titania sent me to ask for your help," said Georgie. "She has found out that Jack Frost is hiding in the human world. The royal seal is drawn towards royalty, so hopefully it will attract Jack Frost to the visiting princes. Will you help me to keep a lookout for it?"

"Yes, of course," said Rachel. "We're going to see the ship launch this morning, so we can start straight away."

Just then, there was a tap on the door. Georgie dived under a lock of Kirsty's hair as the door opened. Mrs Tate popped her head in and smiled at them.

"Good, you're both ready," she said. "Come and have your breakfast, and then we'll set off for the docks."

The girls hurried downstairs to get their breakfast. With a ship launch and a race meeting to attend, and Jack Frost to find, they had a very busy day ahead!

# Making a Splash

Chattering crowds! A marching band! A
seafaring display by the local sea cadets!
The ship docks were so busy and loud
that Rachel and Kirsty couldn't hear
their own voices. They just had to point
at all the things they found interesting –
and there were lots of them! Georgie sat
on Kirsty's shoulder, hidden by her hair.

"Stay close to us," Mr Walker told the girls. "It'd be easy to get lost in this big crowd."

"We've got a good spot here," Mr Tate bellowed over the deafening music. "Look, that platform is where the princes will stand to launch the ship."

A loudspeaker system suddenly crackled into life.

"Now for a marching display by the ship's crew!" a voice announced.

The crew marched out into the area in front of Rachel and Kirsty. The men and women looked very smart…all except one. His uniform was baggy and crumpled, and he kept putting the wrong foot forward and tripping the others up. Kirsty nudged Rachel and mouthed the word "GOBLIN!" at her.

28

Rachel looked at the short figure. His hat was pulled down low over his face and he was wearing white gloves, but he was clearly a goblin. Kirsty felt Georgie squeeze her shoulder.

"He could be carrying the ring for Jack Frost!" she exclaimed.

Just then, the cheers of the crowd seemed to get louder. The reporters' cameras started flashing, and the band struck up a triumphant tune. The princes had arrived!

The first one was about the same age as Rachel and Kirsty, and his name was Prince Alexander. The other two were a few years older, and their names were Prince William and Prince Louis. They all looked very smart.

Rachel was hoping to shake their hands, but just then the goblin left the other crew members and scampered towards the platform. They had to follow him! While everyone was gazing at the princes, Rachel and Kirsty slipped under the barrier and chased the little goblin. He darted out of sight behind the cloth-covered platform and started to climb the steps.

Rachel and Kirsty looked around for a security guard, but everyone was milling around the princes.

"Why is he going up there?" Rachel wondered.

"Whatever it is, I bet he's up to mischief," said Kirsty. "Come on!"

The girls raced up the steps after the goblin. When they reached the top, they saw him pick up a big bottle of champagne, which was tied to a piece of rope.

"That's the bottle they'll smash against the side of the ship to launch it," whispered Rachel. "Dad told me all about the ceremony."

"He's untying the rope!" Kirsty said with a gasp. "Without the bottle, they can't launch the ship. Hey, goblin, STOP!"

The goblin jumped and turned around. When he saw Kirsty and Rachel, he started to back away. He blew a loud raspberry, and suddenly Georgie shot out from under Kirsty's hair.

She zoomed towards the goblin, and
with a cry of alarm he jumped off the
platform and landed in the water with a
huge bellyflop.

Instantly, Georgie waved her wand
and gave the goblin a lifebelt. He floated
slowly over to some steps at the side of
the docks and climbed out, dripping
with muddy water. He looked up at the

girls angrily and shook his fist, before stomping off alone.

"I don't think he had the royal seal," said Georgie. "He just wanted to cause mischief. I'm going to return to Fairyland to see if they have any news there. I'll find you at the racecourse this afternoon."

As Georgie disappeared, the loudspeakers crackled again.

"The launch ceremony is about to start," announced the voice.

Rachel and Kirsty managed to leave the platform without being spotted. Then they hurried back to join their parents as the princes climbed up to the high platform.

Prince Alexander picked up the bottle and swung it against the side of the ship.

35

*SMASH!* Champagne foamed over the big ship.

"I name this ship the *Ocean Princess*," said Prince Alexander. "Bless her and all who sail in her!"

The ship slid smoothly down the slipway and splashed into the water.

Fireworks exploded overhead and the band struck up a merry tune.

"What a wonderful sight!" exclaimed Mr Walker, his eyes shining.

"But now we have to go and catch the train," said Mrs Walker. "Next stop, Hatling Racecourse!"

# Hatling Racecourse

"I've been looking forward to this for weeks!" said Mrs Tate.

She and Mrs Walker were wearing very big, very fancy hats. They couldn't turn around without hitting someone! Mr Tate and Mr Walker thought they looked extremelly funny.

Rachel and Kirsty were given permission to watch the horses walking

around the paddock before the royal
race. They ran down to the paddock
feeling very excited. The Queen's horse
would be running in the race, and the
visiting princes would be there to watch
from the royal box.

A dark-brown stallion was being
paraded past. He had a smooth coat and
a silvery white mark on his forehead in
the shape of a tiny star.

"I think that's Silver Blaze, the Queen's horse," said Kirsty. "Look, he has a crown embossed on his saddle."

"I hope he wins," said Rachel. "It would be wonderful for the visiting princes to see how fast the royal horse can run!"

The girls decided that Silver Blaze was their favourite. Soon the jockeys mounted the horses and rode up to the starting posts, while Rachel and Kirsty followed them.

"Ladies and gentlemen, the royal race will begin in five minutes," said the announcer. "We have two last-minute entries – Snowball and Icicle."

Rachel pointed at a brown stallion and a grey mare trotting along after the others.

"Those must be the late entries," she said. "Goodness, what tiny jockeys!"

The figures on the horses seemed even smaller than the girls. Their riding hats came down very low over their faces, and all the girls could see were two long noses.

"Jockeys are always really small," said Kirsty doubtfully.

"Not *that* small," said Rachel in a worried voice. "Oh, Kirsty, do you think they could be goblins?"

Kirsty checked her watch.

"Only three minutes until the race begins," she said with a groan. "What are we going to do?"

Just then, they walked past a large lady with a very flowery hat. Kirsty looked up at it and gasped. Georgie was sitting on the top, holding onto a large white rose!

"Thank goodness!" said Rachel.

Georgie zoomed down and hid under Kirsty's hair. When the girls explained about the jockeys, Georgie pursed her lips.

"This is bad," she said. "If the goblins spoil the race then the princes will have a terrible time, and one of my jobs is to look after them and make sure they're happy."

Kirsty felt sorry for the little fairy.

"We can't stop the race, but maybe we can still stop the goblins causing trouble," she said. "When we helped the Baby Animal Rescue Fairies, they lent us their ability to talk to animals. Could you give us the ability to talk to horses for a short time? Perhaps if we can talk to the goblins' horses, they'll be able to help us."

"That's a great idea," said Rachel.

Georgie nodded and checked that
no one was looking. Then she waved
her wand, and crown-shaped fairy dust
showered the girls like confetti. They felt
themselves
shrinking, and
wriggled their
shoulders
happily as
their wings
appeared.

"Let's go!"
said Rachel.

They zoomed over
to the starting gates, where the horses
were pawing the ground, eager to start
the race. Rachel dived into Snowball's
brown mane, while Kirsty tucked herself
next to Icicle's grey ear.

"Listen carefully," Kirsty whispered. "I'm a fairy. Your jockey is a naughty goblin, and he's going to try to spoil the race."

"Goblin?" whinnied Icicle in alarm. "Help! Help!"

She kicked the side of the stall. Kirsty heard the goblin give a squawk of alarm.

"It's OK," said Kirsty, trying to sound soothing. "He's much smaller than you and he can't hurt you. All you have to do is take control and not do anything your jockey says."

"Ooh, but I always do what the jockey says," wailed Icicle. "I don't know if I can race by myself."

"Of course you can," said Kirsty in a firm voice. "Be brave."

"Stay with me?" Icicle begged.

Kirsty agreed. She had to make sure that the race went well. An official raised the starting flag.

"We'll be off any second now," said Icicle. "Hold on tight, little fairy!"

In the next stall, Rachel was finding it hard to make Snowball listen at all. He was a very proud and boisterous horse, and he kept shaking his mane and snorting loudly. Rachel saw the starting flag rise into the air and groaned.

"Please listen!" she said for the fifth time.

"I only listen to the drumming of my hooves on the grass!" snorted Snowball, shaking his mane again. "I am the fastest horse in the world!"

"But your jockey is—"

"I don't even need a jockey, I'm so good at racing," Snowball boasted.

"You're absolutely right," said Rachel quickly. "You should do exactly what you want, and show the princes how wonderful you are."

Before Snowball could say anything else, the starting flag swooshed down, the stalls crashed open and the race began!

Rachel and Kirsty twisted their hands into the manes and hung on as tightly as they could. Around the first bend, Icicle's

goblin tugged on her reins to make her
go the wrong way, but she ignored him.
At the second bend, Snowball's goblin
dug in his heels to make him lurch
sideways, but Snowball took no notice.

"Stop running!" Kirsty heard Icicle's
goblin yell. "Do what you're told, stupid
horse!"

"Let me off!" wailed Snowball's goblin.
"I'm going to be sick!"

As they drew closer to the finish line, Snowball and Silver Blaze were neck and neck.

"Come on, Snowball!" cried Rachel. "You can do it!"

"I feel dizzy!" the goblin complained. "My head hurts!"

Just then, Rachel saw Prince William stand up and shout Silver Blaze's name. The Queen's horse gave an extra burst of energy, and crossed the finish line half a second ahead of Snowball!

The crowds went wild, cheering and shouting in delight. Even the princes jumped out of their seats and clapped their hands.

"You were wonderful, Snowball," said Rachel in the horse's ear.

"Yes, I was, wasn't I?" said Snowball, tossing his head. "Of course, I had to let Silver Blaze win. It wasn't good manners to beat the Queen's horse with the princes watching."

Rachel smiled as she fluttered away to join Kirsty and Georgie.

"Well done, you two!" said Georgie. "The princes had a wonderful time."

"I'm afraid the goblins didn't," said Kirsty with a smile.

They watched as the goblin jockeys slithered down to the ground and walked away on wobbly legs.

"We didn't get the chance to check if they were carrying the seal," said Rachel.

"That's what I came to tell you," said Georgie. "Queen Titania has used her magic to find out that Jack Frost is carrying it himself!"

"Then we have to find him," said Kirsty with a gulp.

"Right now you have to return to your normal size and find your parents," said Georgie. "But I'll see you tomorrow. After all, you're going to be at the palace. What better place to look for the royal seal?"

# Garden Goblins

Next day, Mr and Mrs Tate drove Rachel
and Kirsty to the palace. They stopped
at the palace gates, and the girls climbed
out. They were really excited.

"I can't wait to see the princes again,"
said Kirsty, smoothing down her yellow
dress.

"I just hope that we can stop Jack Frost
before he spoils things," said Rachel, as a
palace guard walked over to them.

The guard was wearing a tall, furry hat and a heavy uniform. The girls said goodbye to Mr and Mrs Tate, and then followed him towards the palace. He walked stiffly with his back held very straight, and he didn't speak to them at all.

"I bet those hats get really hot on sunny days," said Kirsty.

Rachel giggled, then gave a squeak of surprise. Georgie was peeping out from under the back of the hat!

She fluttered over to the girls and tucked herself into Rachel's shoulder bag.

"This is the last official event for the princes," said Georgie in a low voice. "If the royal seal has been drawn to them, this is our last chance to find it."

The stern guard led them into the palace gardens. There were children everywhere – walking around the gravel pathways and playing hide-and-seek among the animal-shaped bushes.

Waiters and waitresses were walking around the garden with snacks and drinks. Rachel and Kirsty each took a glass of orange juice and a scone.

"Look over there," said Rachel. "The princes are having scones too."

The princes were sitting at a small round table, sipping tea and eating scones with jam and cream.

"That person looks very interested in the princes," said Kirsty, pointing.

Someone was sitting on a bench under a tree, gazing at the princes, wearing a long, flowery dress that trailed on the ground with two bony feet sticking out.

"I recognise those feet," said Rachel in a low voice. "Kirsty, I'm sure that's Jack Frost!"

They put down their drinks and slipped behind the tree. Just then, three suspiciously short guests wearing large hats came hurrying up. They stood in front of Jack Frost, blocking his view of the princes.

"Goblins!" whispered Georgie, popping her head out of Rachel's bag.

"Do we still have to wear these dresses?" one of the goblins complained.

"Yes," Jack Frost snapped. "Now get out of my way. I can't see the princes! How

am I supposed to learn how to be royal without watching them?"

The goblins raced off, bumping into waiters and waitresses, and sending cakes and drinks flying through the air. They were being a terrible nuisance.

Rachel and Kirsty saw Jack Frost rest his hand on the arm of the bench. Something glimmered on his forefinger, and the girls leaned closer. Georgie gave a squeak of excitement.

"It's the royal seal!" she whispered.

"But how can we get it back?" asked Rachel.

"We might be able to trick him into giving it to us," said Kirsty. "I think I've got an idea. Georgie, I need you to dress us up like the Queen's guards and give us a security scanner."

Puzzled, Georgie waved her wand and the girls found themselves in uniform. They were each wearing a large, furry hat, just like the guards. Rachel was holding a scanner, which was about the same size as a telephone.

The girls walked around the tree and tapped Jack Frost on the shoulder.

"We are doing a security check," said Kirsty in her deepest voice. "We need to scan you. Follow us."

Jack Frost looked cross,

but he followed the girls to a secluded part of the garden, where no one else could see them. Rachel swept the scanner over him, just like she had seen at the airport when she went on holiday.

*BEEEEEP!*

Jack Frost jumped, and Rachel had to stifle a giggle.

"Please take off any metal items," she said.

"Why should I?" Jack Frost demanded.

Rachel didn't know what to say, but Kirsty kept her cool.

"Because if you don't, we will ask you to leave the garden party," she said.

Grumbling crossly, Jack Frost pulled the royal seal off his finger. Rachel held out her hand, and Jack Frost dropped the ring into it.

Instantly, Georgie zoomed to Rachel's side and took the ring, which returned to fairy-size. The girls' disguises disappeared, and Jack Frost's mouth fell open.

"You tricksy, interfering girls!" he bellowed. "I'll make you sorry! Goblins, do your worst!"

"Oh no you don't!" said Georgie.

With a wave of her wand, a tall thorn bush sprang up around the goblins. The girls could hear their muffled squawks.

"They can stay in there until after the garden party," said Georgie to Jack Frost. "Unless you want to use your magic to take them back to the Ice Castle?"

Jack Frost was too angry to speak. He shook his fist at Georgie, and then disappeared in a flash of blue lightning with his goblins.

"We did it!" Georgie exclaimed.

Rachel and Kirsty shared a hug, and Georgie did a somersault in the air. Then they heard a very familiar voice behind them.

"I don't remember having a thorn bush in my garden."

It was the Queen!

# The Newest Prince

The Queen was wearing a sparkly necklace and a delicate peach-coloured silk dress. The girls curtseyed, and Rachel cleared her throat.

"Thorn bushes grow very quickly, Your Majesty," she said. "Perhaps you've never noticed it before."

The Queen gave a little smile. If she had turned her head slightly she would have seen Georgie, but she kept looking the other way.

"I was probably mistaken," the Queen went on, turning away from the thorn bush. "I expect that it will be gone next time I look."

Rachel glanced at Georgie, who gave her wand a little flick. The thorn bush vanished into thin air.

"I will leave you to explore the gardens," said the Queen. "I was a little concerned about some of my *greener* guests, but I believe everything is going smoothly now."

Her eyes twinkled, and the girls curtseyed again. When they looked up, the Queen had gone. Georgie fluttered over to them.

"Thank you both from the bottom of my heart," she said. "Now we can hold the naming ceremony!"

A waterfall of fairy dust sprinkled down on Rachel and Kirsty. The garden around them faded, and the next instant they were standing in the throne room of the Fairyland Palace.

Rachel and Kirsty fluttered their wings and gazed around in delight. The throne room was packed with chattering fairies, the king and queen were sitting on their thrones, and Prince Arthur and Princess Grace were standing beside them. To one side was a beautiful crib, decorated

with delicate lace, filmy frills and white
ribbons. Alexandra the Royal Baby Fairy
was next to the crib, her eyes shining
with happiness.

Queen Titania clapped her hands and
the room fell silent.

"Now that our honoured guests,
Rachel and Kirsty, have saved the royal
seal, we can begin," she said. "We are

here today to welcome a very special
fairy. I am delighted to present... Prince
George!"

Everyone cheered and clapped. Then
Ruby the Red Fairy stepped out of the
crowd and walked over to the crib.

"I give you the gift of making friends
easily," she said, waving her wand over
the baby prince.

Georgie turned and whispered to
Rachel and Kirsty.

"It's Fairyland tradition that each
group of fairies gives the royal baby a
special gift," she said.

Just then, the door banged open and
Jack Frost stomped in, frowning. He sat
down and folded his arms across his chest.

"I think he's had enough of royalty!"
said Rachel with a giggle.

The girls watched the precious magical gifts being presented to the prince. The Music Fairies gave him a beautiful singing voice. The Baby Animal Rescue Fairies gave him the ability to talk to animals. Every group of fairies had something wonderful to add.

When all the gifts had been given, King Oberon held up a large scroll.

"This is Prince George's naming certificate," he said. "To make it official, I ask Georgie the Royal Prince Fairy to stamp it with her royal seal."

Georgie pressed the royal seal against the certificate, and it left a dazzling golden mark. Everyone cheered and clapped.

Amid the celebrations, Rachel and Kirsty tiptoed over to the royal crib.

The tiny prince was now fast asleep, and his gauzy blue wings were folded around his little body like a delicate swaddling blanket.

"He's the sweetest little baby I've ever seen," she said.

"Isn't it amazing to think that we've helped to welcome him into the world?" asked Kirsty, squeezing her best friend's hand.

Rachel nodded and looked at Kirsty with a smile.

"Those visiting princes have a very exciting life," she said. "But I wouldn't swap places with them for the world!"

Now it's time for Kirsty and
Rachel to help...

# Kayla the Pottery Fairy

**Read on for a sneak peek...**

"I can see Rainspell Island!" Rachel
cried as the ferry sailed across the blue-
green sea, foamy waves slapping against
its sides. Ahead of them was a rocky
island with soaring cliffs and crescents of
golden sandy beaches around the coast.
"Not far now, Kirsty."

"Aren't we lucky, Rachel?" Kirsty said,
her face alight with excitement. "We
came here not long ago for the music
festival, and now we're back again for
Craft Week!"

"And maybe some fairy adventures,
too?" Rachel murmured hopefully.

"Maybe, if we're *very* lucky," said Kirsty with a smile. ..

Read **Kayla the Pottery Fairy** to find out what adventures are in store for Kirsty and Rachel!

Join in the magic online by signing up to the Rainbow Magic fan club!

Sign up today at:
www.rainbowmagicbooks.co.uk

# Pick your favourite royal story!

# Competition!

Georgie the Royal Prince Fairy has created
a special competition just for you!
All you need to do is answer the question below.
When you have the answer, go online and enter!

We will put all the correct entries into a draw and select a winner
to receive a special Rainbow Magic goodie bag with lots
of treats for you and your fairy friends.
We'll even name a character in a new Rainbow Magic
story after you!

**What is the name of the racecourse
that Kirsty and Rachel visit
in Georgie the Royal Prince Fairy?**

_ _ _ _ _ _ _ _

# Enter online now at www.rainbowmagicbooks.co.uk

No purchase required. Entrants must sign up to the Rainbow Magic newsletter to enter.
Only one entry per child. One prize draw will take place on 31st July 2014 and
one on 31st October 2014. Alternatively readers can send the answer on a postcard to:
Rainbow Magic, Georgie the Royal Prince Fairy Competition,
Orchard Books, 338 Euston Road, London, NW1 3BH. Australian readers can write to:
Rainbow Magic, Georgie the Royal Prince Fairy Competition,
Hachette Children's Books, Level 17/207 Kent St, Sydney, NSW 2000.
E-mail: childrens.books@hachette.com.au.
New Zealand readers should write to: Rainbow Magic, Georgie the Royal Prince Fairy
Competition, 4 Whetu Place, Mairangi Bay, Auckland, NZ

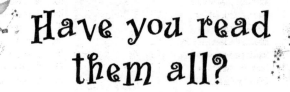

# Have you read them all?

**The Rainbow Fairies**
1. Ruby the Red Fairy ☐
2. Amber the Orange Fairy ☐
3. Saffron the Yellow Fairy ☐
4. Fern the Green Fairy ☐
5. Sky the Blue Fairy ☐
6. Izzy the Indigo Fairy ☐
7. Heather the Violet Fairy ☐

**The Weather Fairies**
8. Crystal the Snow Fairy ☐
9. Abigail the Breeze Fairy ☐
10. Pearl the Cloud Fairy ☐
11. Goldie the Sunshine Fairy ☐
12. Evie the Mist Fairy ☐
13. Storm the Lightning Fairy ☐
14. Hayley the Rain Fairy ☐

**The Party Fairies**
15. Cherry the Cake Fairy ☐
16. Melodie the Music Fairy ☐
17. Grace the Glitter Fairy ☐
18. Honey the Sweet Fairy ☐
19. Polly the Party Fun Fairy ☐
20. Phoebe the Fashion Fairy ☐
21. Jasmine the Present Fairy ☐

**The Jewel Fairies**
22. India the Moonstone Fairy ☐
23. Scarlett the Garnet Fairy ☐
24. Emily the Emerald Fairy ☐
25. Chloe the Topaz Fairy ☐
26. Amy the Amethyst Fairy ☐
27. Sophie the Sapphire Fairy ☐
28. Lucy the Diamond Fairy ☐

**The Pet Keeper Fairies**
29. Katie the Kitten Fairy ☐
30. Bella the Bunny Fairy ☐
31. Georgia the Guinea Pig Fairy ☐
32. Lauren the Puppy Fairy ☐
33. Harriet the Hamster Fairy ☐
34. Molly the Goldfish Fairy ☐
35. Penny the Pony Fairy ☐

**The Fun Day Fairies**
36. Megan the Monday Fairy ☐
37. Tallulah the Tuesday Fairy ☐
38. Willow the Wednesday Fairy ☐
39. Thea the Thursday Fairy ☐
40. Freya the Friday Fairy ☐
41. Sienna the Saturday Fairy ☐
42. Sarah the Sunday Fairy ☐

**The Petal Fairies**
43. Tia the Tulip Fairy ☐
44. Pippa the Poppy Fairy ☐
45. Louise the Lily Fairy ☐
46. Charlotte the Sunflower Fairy ☐
47. Olivia the Orchid Fairy ☐
48. Danielle the Daisy Fairy ☐
49. Ella the Rose Fairy ☐

**The Dance Fairies**
50. Bethany the Ballet Fairy ☐
51. Jade the Disco Fairy ☐
52. Rebecca the Rock'n'Roll Fairy ☐
53. Tasha the Tap Dance Fairy ☐
54. Jessica the Jazz Fairy ☐
55. Saskia the Salsa Fairy ☐
56. Imogen the Ice Dance Fairy ☐

**The Sporty Fairies**
57. Helena the Horseriding Fairy ☐
58. Francesca the Football Fairy ☐
59. Zoe the Skating Fairy ☐
60. Naomi the Netball Fairy ☐
61. Samantha the Swimming Fairy ☐
62. Alice the Tennis Fairy ☐
63. Gemma the Gymnastics Fairy ☐

**The Music Fairies**
64. Poppy the Piano Fairy ☐
65. Ellie the Guitar Fairy ☐
66. Fiona the Flute Fairy ☐
67. Danni the Drum Fairy ☐
68. Maya the Harp Fairy ☐
69. Victoria the Violin Fairy ☐
70. Sadie the Saxophone Fairy ☐

## The Magical Animal Fairies

71. Ashley the Dragon Fairy ☐
72. Lara the Black Cat Fairy ☐
73. Erin the Firebird Fairy ☐
74. Rihanna the Seahorse Fairy ☐
75. Sophia the Snow Swan Fairy ☐
76. Leona the Unicorn Fairy ☐
77. Caitlin the Ice Bear Fairy ☐

## The Green Fairies

78. Nicole the Beach Fairy ☐
79. Isabella the Air Fairy ☐
80. Edie the Garden Fairy ☐
81. Coral the Reef Fairy ☐
82. Lily the Rainforest Fairy ☐
83. Carrie the Snow Cap Fairy ☐
84. Milly the River Fairy ☐

## The Ocean Fairies

85. Ally the Dolphin Fairy ☐
86. Amelie the Seal Fairy ☐
87. Pia the Penguin Fairy ☐
88. Tess the Sea Turtle Fairy ☐
89. Stephanie the Starfish Fairy ☐
90. Whitney the Whale Fairy ☐
91. Courtney the Clownfish Fairy ☐

## The Twilight Fairies

92. Ava the Sunset Fairy ☐
93. Lexi the Firefly Fairy ☐
94. Zara the Starlight Fairy ☐
95. Morgan the Midnight Fairy ☐
96. Yasmin the Night Owl Fairy ☐
97. Maisie the Moonbeam Fairy ☐
98. Sabrina the Sweet Dreams Fairy ☐

## The Showtime Fairies

99. Madison the Magic Show Fairy ☐
100. Leah the Theatre Fairy ☐
101. Alesha the Acrobat Fairy ☐
102. Darcey the Dance Diva Fairy ☐
103. Taylor the Talent Show Fairy ☐
104. Amelia the Singing Fairy ☐
105. Isla the Ice Star Fairy ☐

## The Princess Fairies

106. Honor the Happy Days Fairy ☐
107. Demi the Dressing-Up Fairy ☐
108. Anya the Cuddly Creatures Fairy ☐
109. Elisa the Adventure Fairy ☐
110. Lizzie the Sweet Treats Fairy ☐
111. Maddie the Playtime Fairy ☐
112. Eva the Enchanted Ball Fairy ☐

## The Pop Star Fairies

113. Jessie the Lyrics Fairy ☐
114. Adele the Singing Coach Fairy ☐
115. Vanessa the Dance Steps Fairy ☐
116. Miley the Stylist Fairy ☐
117. Frankie the Make-Up Fairy ☐
118. Rochelle the Star Spotter Fairy ☐
119. Una the Concert Fairy ☐

## The Fashion Fairies

120. Miranda the Beauty Fairy ☐
121. Claudia the Accessories Fairy ☐
122. Tyra the Dress Designer Fairy ☐
123. Alexa the Fashion Reporter Fairy ☐
124. Matilda the Hair Stylist Fairy ☐
125. Brooke the Photographer Fairy ☐
126. Lola the Fashion Fairy ☐

## The Sweet Fairies

127. Lottie the Lollipop Fairy ☐
128. Esme the Ice Cream Fairy ☐
129. Coco the Cupcake Fairy ☐
130. Clara the Chocolate Fairy ☐
131. Madeleine the Cookie Fairy ☐
132. Layla the Candyfloss Fairy ☐
133. Nina the Birthday Cake Fairy ☐

## The Baby Animal Rescue Fairies

134. Mae the Panda Fairy ☐
135. Kitty the Tiger Fairy ☐
136. Mara the Meerkat Fairy ☐
137. Savannah the Zebra Fairy ☐
138. Kimberley the Koala Fairy ☐
139. Rosie the Honey Bear Fairy ☐
140. Anna the Arctic Fox Fairy ☐

## The Magical Crafts Fairies

141. Kayla the Pottery Fairy ☐
142. Annabelle the Drawing Fairy ☐
143. Zadie the Sewing Fairy ☐
144. Josie the Jewellery Fairy ☐
145. Violet the Painting Fairy ☐
146. Libby the Story-Writing Fairy ☐
147. Roxie the Baking Fairy ☐

There's a book of fairy fun for everyone!

# www.rainbowmagicbooks.co.uk

# Lila & Myla the Twins Fairies

Meet Lila and Myla the Twins Fairies!
Can the fairies trick Jack Frost before he uses
their magic to create his very own twin?

www.rainbowmagicbooks.co.uk